THE PUPPY PLACE

CUDDLES

Don't miss any of these other stories by Ellen Miles!

THE PUPPY PLACE

CUDDLES

ELLEN MILES

SCHOLASTIC INC.

Copyright © 2018 by Ellen Miles
Cover art by Tim O'Brien
Original cover design by Steve Scott

ISBN 978-1-338-30300-1

10 9 8 7 6 5 4 3 2   18 19 20 21 22 23

Printed in the U.S.A.   40
First printing 2019

For all the puppies who give the best cuddles when we need them

CHAPTER ONE

"Hi, Misha, hi!" Lizzie Peterson squatted down to pet the wriggly, panting husky. The dog hardly knew her, but like most dogs, he was always happy to see a friendly person. She ruffled the thick white fur around Misha's neck and gazed into his blue eyes. "How's my handsome boy?" she asked.

He grinned a doggy grin at her and wriggled some more, wagging his fluffy tail hard. Lizzie could tell that he was about to jump on her, so she distracted him by standing up. "Sit," she told him as she gave a hand signal.

Misha sat.

Now his tail swept the floor as he wagged, still grinning up at her.

Lizzie laughed. The best thing about her job was the happy dogs. Lizzie and her best friend, Maria, and two other girls—Daphne and Brianna—had a dog-walking business. They took care of dogs for people who wanted their pets to have a little extra attention and exercise. Lizzie loved to help with training, too; she was the one who had taught Misha how to sit, and she was planning to work more on his jumping-up issue.

Every day—at least, every school day—her clients' dogs waited patiently for her to arrive. And when she did, every single dog behaved as if she was the best thing that had happened all day. She was greeted with wags and wriggles, kisses and excited barks. It always felt great.

"It's so easy to make you guys happy," Lizzie

told Misha as she looked for his leash. "A few pats, maybe a treat, and you've made a new bestie. Now, where do they keep your stuff?"

Misha was not one of Lizzie's regular charges. Normally, he was on Daphne's route. Lizzie was covering for Daphne, who wanted a few afternoons off because her aunt was visiting from Colorado. "Please?" Daphne had asked. "She's my favorite aunt, and I never get to see her. She wants to take me shopping and to the movies and stuff."

Lizzie didn't mind. She liked meeting new dogs and visiting with ones she had met before, like Misha. She just wished Daphne kept better notes on the dogs she walked. Lizzie checked the index card she had pulled out of her pocket. *Misha*, it said. *Husky, six years old. Pulls on leash. Very strong. Likes to chase squirrels.* All of that was helpful—but pretty predictable, if you knew anything about huskies. Lizzie also really needed to know what commands Misha had been taught, whether he was allowed to eat just any dog treats or if he was allergic to wheat or anything else, and . . . "And where is your leash?" she asked Misha.

Misha pranced to a cabinet near the front door and put a paw on it. Lizzie laughed again. "It's in there?" she asked. "Are you sure?"

Misha took a few steps back, sat down, and *woo-woo*ed, throwing his head back to let out a few soft, short howls. Lizzie loved the *woo-woo* huskies did instead of barking. Once she'd even met a husky who had been trained to say "I love you" in howls. It sounded more like "Wyyy wuuuuuvvvv wooooooohhh!" and it was hilarious.

Lizzie pulled the cabinet door open. "Yes!" she said. There it was, a handsome red leather leash hanging on a hook. "Good boy. You do know where your leash is, don't you?" She took the leash out and snapped it onto Misha's collar. "Great, now we can go." She knew she had everything else she might need in her backpack: dog treats (she always carried wheat-free ones just in case a client's dog did turn out to be allergic), a bottle of water, poop clean-up bags, and even a doggy emergency kit with bandages and other supplies.

She had gotten the kit when she took a course on canine first aid at the community center. There Lizzie had learned to bandage paws, clean cuts, and even do doggy CPR, helping an unconscious dog with his breathing. Fortunately, so far she had not had to use anything she'd learned, except once, when her own puppy, Buddy, cut his foot on a piece of broken glass.

Poor little Buddy. Lizzie pictured her sweet brown puppy looking up at her with the saddest eyes as he held out his bleeding paw. She smiled as she remembered how he'd licked her cheek in thanks when she was done cleaning and bandaging the cut.

Buddy had first come to the Petersons' as a foster puppy. Lizzie's family had fostered many puppies before and after Buddy, keeping each one just long enough to find it the perfect home — but Buddy was the only one who had come to stay. The whole family — Lizzie, her parents, and her two younger brothers, Charles and the Bean — had fallen madly in love with the adorable mixed-breed pup. There was no question that Buddy was their favorite puppy ever.

"But I do like you, too, Misha," Lizzie told the husky. He was prancing around now, still wearing that silly grin. She knew he was more than ready for his walk. "Let's go, then," she said as they headed out the back door together.

"Misha, Misha!" Lizzie heard a girl's voice. Misha heard the voice, too. He strained at his leash, towing Lizzie toward the sidewalk.

He dragged her straight for a small wiry girl with her bright red hair done in two braids. She looked a little younger than Lizzie—*probably a first-grader*, Lizzie thought. The girl must have been playing in the yard next door, where Lizzie spotted a swing set. Her freckles and those long red braids reminded Lizzie of Pippi Longstocking, the feisty main character in one of Lizzie's favorite books.

Before Lizzie could even think of the best way to slow him down, Misha pulled her right up to the girl. The girl laughed and thumped him and petted him and stroked his long, fluffy tail. "Misha, Misha," she said again. "Good boy, Misha." She giggled as he licked her face.

Then the girl stopped to stare at Lizzie. "Who are you?" she asked.

Lizzie smiled. "I'm Lizzie. I'm taking over for Daphne this week. Who are you?"

"I'm Poppy," said the girl. "I know Daphne. I've gone with her on her dog walks. Can I come with you?"

"If your mom says yes, sure!" said Lizzie.

The girl grinned. "Really? I live right there," she said, pointing to the big white house next door to Misha's.

"Okay, well, let's ask her," said Lizzie.

Poppy's mom came to the door when Poppy called for her. She had red hair, too, but hers was cut short, with bangs.

"Hi," Lizzie said. "I'm Lizzie Peterson. I'm the president of the dog-walking business your neighbor Daphne works for."

The woman looked surprised. "Funny, somehow I always thought Daphne was the president," she said.

Lizzie smiled. "That's interesting," she said. "Anyway, is it okay if Poppy walks with me? I'm just going around the block, and I'm used to watching kids."

"How about if I come along?" The woman stuck out her hand. "I'm Allie. Allie Bauer."

"Great," said Lizzie. She checked the list Daphne had left for her. "Next stop is to pick up Ruby."

Allie shook her head. "Nope, next stop is Cuddles."

Again Lizzie checked Daphne's sheet, with all her clients' names and addresses. "I don't see a Cuddles on Daphne's list," she said.

"Oh, Daphne doesn't walk her," said Allie.

"Poppy just loves to visit her. Poor little puppy, left all alone all day."

Before Lizzie had a chance to ask more, she heard noises. A bark, a whimper, a whine. The puppy was not far off—and she was not happy. "Let's go," said Lizzie.

CHAPTER TWO

Lizzie and Allie walked down the sidewalk toward a small green house. Poppy trotted along next to Misha, petting his head and talking to him as they walked.

"Good boy, Misha," the little girl said. "What do you smell?"

Misha cocked his head from side to side, grinning up at her as she questioned him. He held his tail high, and his collar tags jingled a happy tune as he walked. Lizzie smiled at Allie. "Poppy seems to really love dogs," she said.

Allie sighed. "It's more than that," she said. "She's totally dog-crazy. She's dying for a dog of her own, but now is not the time. Our lives are just way too busy and full. There's no room for a dog right now. Plus, I'm a bit allergic, so it wouldn't be easy to find the right dog for us."

Lizzie nodded. "It's a serious decision, to get a dog," she said, echoing something she'd heard Ms. Dobbins say. "It's definitely a lot of responsibility. Not every family is ready for a pet." Lizzie knew about that from volunteering at her local animal shelter, Caring Paws, where Ms. Dobbins was the director. She knew of more than one pet who had ended up at Caring Paws when its family felt too overwhelmed with busy schedules.

Allie shook her head. "Exactly. Maybe someday we'll be ready, but not now."

The puppy noises had gotten much louder. Lizzie could hardly hear Allie over the barking, whining, and yipping that came from the screened-in porch of the green house.

At first Lizzie didn't see a dog. Then she saw a fluffy little head pop up as a dog jumped high enough to peep over the porch railing. She heard scrabbling noises, and then the head popped up at the other end of the porch. The dog ran back and forth, bouncing up and down so it could peek out.

"Hi, Cuddles!" Poppy said.

"Whoa, that is the most adorable dog!" Lizzie said. She grinned at Allie, then turned back to catch another glimpse. Lizzie thought she knew all her dog breeds—she studied the "Dog Breeds of the World" poster in her room every night—but she'd never seen one quite like this. It looked sort of like a Pomeranian: small, with fluffy reddish-brown fur. But instead of a pointy nose, this dog had a broad one, and its shiny round black eyes were more widely spaced. The dog's furry face and cute ears looked familiar, and suddenly

Lizzie realized why. It looked exactly like Bosco, the Bean's favorite teddy bear. She turned to say so to Allie. "She looks just like a—"

"Teddy bear!" said Poppy. "That's what she is. I looked it up online. She's a teddy bear dog. It's a mixed breed, what they call a designer dog."

Lizzie raised her eyebrows. She didn't meet too many people who knew more about dogs than she did. "Interesting," she said, nodding.

Poppy pointed to the bouncing puppy. "I don't know if they're all as bouncy as this one, but I guess she can't help it. She's all cooped up on that porch."

"What do you mean?" asked Lizzie.

"She's only lived here for about a week," explained Allie, "but she's out there all day every day. I don't know what Mrs. Bennett was thinking. She's never home. Why did she get a dog if she can't spend any time with her?"

As Allie and Lizzie talked, the dog began to calm down a bit. Misha was calm, too. The husky stood quietly on the sidewalk as Poppy stroked his back.

"It's okay, Cuddles," said Poppy. "We're your friends."

Lizzie laughed. "Cuddles. It sure suits her. I'm sure everyone who sees her wants to cuddle with her. How do you know her name, anyway?" she asked.

"I heard the lady yelling at her to stop barking," said Poppy.

Lizzie felt her heart thumping. She wanted to run right up to that porch and take Cuddles along with them on their walk. She hated to see a dog left alone like that. Dogs just wanted to be with people and other dogs. It wasn't fair to get a dog if you didn't have time to spend walking and playing with it.

Allie must have seen the look on Lizzie's face. "I know," she said. "Poor dog, right? But there's not really anything we can do."

Lizzie frowned. "Maybe there is," she said. "What did you say her owner's name is?"

"Mrs. Bennett," said Allie.

Lizzie shrugged off her backpack. "I'm going to leave her a note," she said. "Maybe she'd like AAA Dynamic Dog Walkers to help her out with Cuddles." She rummaged for a pen and paper, then dug one of her business cards out of the backpack's side pocket. She showed it to Allie and Poppy. "See? There's Daphne, and also Brianna, and my best friend, Maria. We take care of lots of dogs." Lizzie loved the picture of all four of them with some of their favorite clients: dogs of every size, shape, and color. In the picture, Lizzie was holding one dog in her arms (Maxx, a mini Doberman pinscher) and two on leashes (Pixie and Pogo, a pair of poodles). Maria sat on the grass with three puppies trying to get into her lap at the same time while Brianna wrangled a high-spirited golden retriever. "Look, Daphne's holding Misha in the picture!" Lizzie pointed out the handsome husky, and Poppy smiled.

Lizzie scribbled a note to Mrs. Bennett. Then she glanced at Poppy. The girl was small, but she looked strong. "Can you hold Misha's leash for a second?" Lizzie asked.

Poppy nodded eagerly. She took the leash and carefully wrapped it around her hand. "Sit, Misha," she said. Misha sat.

Lizzie was impressed. This girl had a way with dogs.

"Okay?" Lizzie asked.

"Okay," said Poppy.

Allie smiled and winked at Lizzie.

Lizzie walked up to the door of the screened porch and knocked. The puppy went wild, but that was it. Nobody came to the door or called out, "Who's there?"

"Nobody home," said Lizzie. She stuck the business card and her note into the screen door. Cuddles yipped louder than ever until Lizzie shushed her with calming words. Lizzie put her palm against the screen, and Cuddles snuffled at her fingers. "It's okay," Lizzie told Cuddles. "Don't worry. We'll get you out of there one way or another."

CHAPTER THREE

Lizzie called Daphne as soon as she got home.

"I can only talk for a minute," said Daphne. "My aunt and I are baking cookies and they're just about to come out of the oven."

"What's up with Cuddles, that little barking dog on the porch of the green house?" Lizzie asked, getting straight to the point.

"Exactly!" said Daphne. "What *is* up over there? Poor thing. I've been knocking on the door every day, but nobody's ever home. That dog needs some training to learn how to keep quiet."

"Almost any dog would bark if they were left alone like that," said Lizzie. "She's bored and frustrated and lonely. It's like dogs who are tied out all day on a run. A lot of them bark, too. But if they're treated right and have time with their humans, they don't bark at all."

"Okay, whatever," said Daphne. Lizzie could tell she was probably rolling her eyes. "Anyway, I have to go. The oven timer just went off and those cookies smell gooo-oood."

"Wait, I wanted to tell you that I met Poppy today. She said she knows you."

"That pest?" Daphne asked. "What a know-it-all. She thinks she knows more about dogs than I do."

Lizzie stifled a giggle. She had a feeling that it could be true. Normally, she might have felt the same way as Daphne—but there was something about Poppy that Lizzie really liked. She said good-bye and hung up. All that evening as she did her homework, ate dinner with her family, and played hide-the-biscuit with Buddy, Lizzie listened for the phone, waiting for a call from Mrs. Bennett. But the phone never rang.

The next afternoon, everything happened just the way it had the day before. Misha met Lizzie at the door again, with wags and grins. Lizzie asked where his leash was, and he put a paw on the cabinet door. "Good boy," she said as she clipped it on.

Poppy called out again as soon as Lizzie and the husky stepped out the door. "Hi, Misha," Poppy said. She fell into step next to Lizzie as she and Misha reached the sidewalk. "Mom said I could go with you today," she said, "as long as we don't cross any streets and if I listen to what you say."

"Great!" said Lizzie. It was always nice to have company on a walk. Lizzie could already hear Cuddles whining and barking. The sounds grew louder as she and Poppy approached the green house. Soon Lizzie could see the little dog racing from end to end of the porch, popping up to peer out at them. Cuddles was frantic! Lizzie felt so sorry for the adorable puppy.

"Hi, Cuddles," Poppy called softly.

The barking did not let up. Lizzie wondered if the poor dog had been on the porch all night. Did she ever get walked at all? Lizzie asked Poppy to hold Misha again, then marched up to the house and knocked loudly on the porch door. She noticed that the business card she had left was gone. So Mrs. Bennett must have at least seen them.

Cuddles barked and barked, but nobody came to the door. Lizzie peered through the screen. For a moment, she thought she saw movement inside, just the twitch of a curtain at a window near the front door. "Hello," she called, knocking again. "Mrs. Bennett?" But there was no answer. Everything was still again—except for Cuddles, who bounced and barked and scrabbled at the door.

Lizzie clenched her fists. "That's it," she said as she rejoined Poppy on the sidewalk. "We've got to do something about this. That dog needs our help."

Poppy nodded. "But what can we do?"

Lizzie sighed. "I don't know," she said. "But I'll think it over while we walk. And maybe your mom will have some ideas." She and Poppy walked around the block, letting Misha sniff every bush and tree along the way. The sound of Cuddles's barking faded as they got farther away, but it grew louder again as they completed their walk and ended up back on the sidewalk in front of the Bauers' house.

Poppy's mom was out front, watering some big red flowers that grew along the front walk. "Hi," Allie called. "Did you have a nice walk?"

"Misha peed seven times!" Poppy reported. "No, eight," she added. "I forgot about the time he went on that mailbox."

"Well, it all sounds very exciting," said Allie, giving Lizzie a wink and a smile.

"And Cuddles barked and barked and barked," added Poppy. "We have to help her."

Allie frowned. "I know. I can hear her from here," she said. "Poor little puppy. I agree, I'd love to help her. But what can we do?"

"I've been thinking about that," said Lizzie. "Do you have Mrs. Bennett's phone number? She never called me last night, so maybe I'll just call her."

"I don't have it, but I bet I can find it," said Allie. "Come on in and have a glass of lemonade while I look it up. Misha is welcome, too." She put down her watering can and headed for the house.

"Don't mind the mess," Allie said as she led Lizzie into the kitchen. "I never seem to catch up." She poured lemonade for all of them, then went straight to the laptop on the crowded counter and began tapping away. "It's great that you want to help Cuddles," she said as she typed.

"It's what I do," Lizzie said. "I mean, it's what my family does. We're a foster family, and we love to take care of puppies who need help."

"Ohh, you're so lucky!" said Poppy.

Allie looked up at Lizzie and smiled. "That's wonderful," she said. "How long do they usually stay with you?"

"Well, some are only with us for a few days," said Lizzie. "But some stay longer. It depends on how long it takes to find the right forever family for each dog. We try to make the right match, like an energetic dog with an athletic person, or a mellow dog with someone who likes to stay in and take it easy."

"Isn't it hard to give up the puppies?" Poppy asked. "Don't you just want to keep them all?"

Lizzie nodded. "Always. But we want them to have good homes, so that's the main thing."

Poppy smiled. "Cool," she said.

Lizzie could have talked about fostering forever, but just then Allie interrupted the conversation. "Hey, guess what?" she said, closing her computer and picking up her phone. "I found Mrs. Bennett's number—and I'm going to call her right now."

CHAPTER FOUR

Allie tapped at her phone, then held it to her ear. After a moment, she let her arm fall to her side. For the first time since Lizzie had met her, she was not smiling. "No answer," she said. "And no answering machine."

"But I'm almost positive someone's home," said Lizzie. She told Allie about seeing movement inside the house.

"Well, then, let's go back there right now," said Allie. She looked around the kitchen and grabbed a box of cookies from a shelf. "We'll pay Mrs. Bennett a neighborly visit."

Lizzie stood up. "Maybe I should take Misha home first, just to make things a little simpler."

"Good idea," said Allie. "We'll meet you out front after you drop him off."

Lizzie took Misha home and gave him a biscuit and a pat good-bye. "See you tomorrow," she told him. "Be a good boy."

Misha gobbled the biscuit before she could take a step, then grinned at her and thumped his tail, asking for another.

"Okay, one more," said Lizzie, handing it over. Then she headed back out to meet Allie and Poppy.

"What grade are you in?" she asked Poppy as they walked. She didn't remember seeing Poppy at their school.

Poppy looked at her mom and smiled. "Well, I'm in fourth grade for reading," she said, "and third grade for math. And I guess I'm like an eighth grader when it comes to science, since I'm studying chemistry."

"Poppy is homeschooled," explained Allie. "She works with an online program, and we also do a lot of outside activities."

"Like helping at the farm with the goats and working with Aunt Kate at the lab," said Poppy. "My aunt's a scientist," she told Lizzie. "I help her with her experiments."

Allie laughed. "Well, mostly we wash bottles and help clean up, but it's a fascinating environment."

"I want to be a scientist when I grow up, too," said Poppy. "Or maybe an astronaut, or both. I'd like to be the first woman on Mars."

"Wow," said Lizzie. She wanted to ask more, but she was distracted by Cuddles's barking and yipping as they got close to the green house. Even from down the block, Lizzie could see her fuzzy little copper-colored ears popping up and down as she ran from one end of the porch to the other.

Allie just shook her head. "Let's go do something about this," she said. She marched right up to the porch and knocked loudly at the door. Cuddles went wild, barking even more and scrabbling at the door.

There was no answer.

Allie looked at Lizzie. "I'm going onto the porch so I can knock on the front door," she said. "Help me make sure the dog doesn't get out." She pushed open the screen door, quickly putting a foot inside to block Cuddles from escaping. Then she reached down and picked the tiny thing up. "Got her!" she said. "Come on in."

Lizzie wouldn't have dared to walk right onto the screened porch, but if a grown-up was doing it, maybe it was okay. She and Poppy followed Allie through the door. Once they were all on the porch, Allie made sure the screen door was shut and put Cuddles down. Immediately, the little pup ran to each of them in turn, putting a paw up on their legs and panting happily as she wagged her fluffy tail.

Company! I love company. I've been so lonely and bored.

Lizzie's heart melted as she watched the puppy greet Poppy, and she reached down to pet Cuddles's soft, fluffy ears. "Hey there," she said.

Allie knocked sharply on the front door. "Hello?" she called. "Mrs. Bennett? We've come to pay a visit."

For a moment, Lizzie thought nobody was going to answer. There was no movement inside, no sound of footsteps. Then the door opened, just a crack at first, and then a little more. "Yes?" asked the frowning woman inside. "What do you want?"

"I'm so sorry to intrude. We don't really want anything—we're just here to pay a visit," said Allie. "And to bring you these." She thrust the box of cookies forward. "I'm your neighbor Allie Bauer. I can't believe we've never met. This is my daughter, Poppy. And this is our friend Lizzie Peterson. She's a professional dog walker."

Mrs. Bennett sniffed. "The one who left advertisements here. I am not interested, thank you very much."

She began to shut the door, but Allie pushed the box of cookies toward her so it was in the way. "Please, we would just like to talk to you for a moment. It's about your dog."

"Not my dog," said Mrs. Bennett. "She's my sister's. Well, she *was* my sister's, until Eleanor moved to Montreal and dumped her with me." She folded her arms. "She made me promise not to let her out of my sight, but I don't know how she thought I was supposed to take care of a dog when I work two jobs just to keep a roof over my head and food on the table."

"That's why we're here," said Lizzie. "We want to help you with Cuddles."

"Can't afford it," said Mrs. Bennett. "Didn't you hear what I just said?" This time she reached for the box of cookies before she began to close the door in their faces.

"Wait!" said Lizzie. "I'll do it for free. I'll walk her and help train her, and if you need me to find a new home for her, I can do that, too."

Slowly, the door opened back up. "For free?" asked Mrs. Bennett, looking at Lizzie suspiciously.

CHAPTER FIVE

"Once she knew I wasn't going to charge her any-thing, Mrs. Bennett turned out to be pretty nice," Lizzie told Maria the next day as they walked toward Misha's house. Lizzie had convinced Maria to come along with her on Daphne's route so she could meet Cuddles, and she had been filling Maria in on the whole story.

"Mrs. Bennett told us how her sister had a teddy bear named Cuddles when they were little," Lizzie said. "That's how Cuddles got her name."

"But then her sister had to give up the dog?" Maria asked.

Lizzie nodded. "Mrs. Bennett promised she would take care of Cuddles," she said. "She's been feeling awful about how little time she has to spend with the dog. She was putting her out on the porch so Cuddles could at least run around a bit and see people going by. She meant well, even if it wasn't really the best idea."

"It sure wasn't," said Maria. "One of Simba's littermates jumped right through a screen door during a thunderstorm one night. She ran off and got lost for five whole days."

Simba was Maria's mother's guide dog. He was a laid-back yellow Lab whose entire focus was on doing his job—although Lizzie knew that he did enjoy belly rubs when he was off duty.

"Well, it's a good thing Cuddles hasn't done that," said Lizzie. "But it's an even better thing that we're going to be able to get her off that porch and take her for walks. I tried to convince Mrs. Bennett to let my family keep Cuddles until we can find another home, but she keeps saying how she promised her sister that she wouldn't let Cuddles out of her sight. So guess I'll sort of be fostering her without actually taking her to live with us."

"I bet Cuddles will be much happier when she gets some exercise and some company," said Maria. "It sounds like that's what she really needs."

The girls stopped to pick up Misha, and when they went outside again, Poppy was waiting for them.

"Hi, Misha," she called. "Hi, Lizzie! Can I come with you again today?"

"Sure," said Lizzie. "This is my friend Maria. She's coming, too."

Maria smiled at Poppy. "So, I hear you like dogs?" she asked as they walked together toward Cuddles's house.

"I love them!" said Poppy. Her whole face lit up. "I'm going to have a hundred dogs when I'm older."

Maria laughed. "You sound like Lizzie," she said. "What's your favorite breed?"

"Well," said Poppy, "I love Labs. But I also like German shepherds and golden retrievers, and huskies like Misha. And I always wanted to have a Great Dane."

This time Lizzie laughed. "You and I really are alike," she said. "I love big dogs, too."

Maria told Poppy about Simba. "Maybe you can meet him someday," she said.

"And Buddy, too," said Lizzie. "He's not a huge dog, but he's the best."

"I wouldn't care what size or breed it was if I could have a dog of my own," said Poppy. "Just a dog to snuggle with, and teach tricks to, and take for walks."

"You will, someday," said Lizzie. She knew how hard it was to want a dog and not be able to have one. She had yearned for a dog for so many years before her family got Buddy. "Meanwhile, maybe you can help us with Cuddles."

Poppy's face lit up again. "I can't wait to take her out for a walk. She's adorable and so cuddly!" she told Maria.

"She is," said Lizzie. "For a little dog, that is." She grinned at Poppy.

A few moments later, they were in front of the green house. Cuddles raced up and down the porch, barking and whining.

"It's okay, Cuddles," said Lizzie. "We're here to take you out."

"Oh, look at her!" said Maria when the little head popped up into view. "She's even cuter than I pictured."

Lizzie handed Misha's leash to Poppy. Then she opened the screen door carefully and stepped inside. Cuddles scampered toward her with a huge grin on her adorable little face.

You're here, you're here! Hurray! Let's have some fun.

Cuddles pranced in figure eights around Lizzie's ankles. Lizzie laughed. "Hold on there, little one," she said. "Let me get your leash on." Finally, she had to pick Cuddles up to calm the little dog. "Aww, what a darling," she said as she nuzzled the soft fur around the puppy's neck. Cuddles hardly weighed a thing. She settled immediately into Lizzie's arms, looking up at her with her sweet brown eyes.

"Okay, sweetie pie," said Lizzie. "Let's go say hi to everyone." She put Cuddles down and led her outside. "Easy now," she said. "Don't scare her!"

Poppy made a face. "I know," she said. But Cuddles wasn't scared. She ran straight to Poppy and let herself be hugged and kissed and cooed over while Maria patiently waited her turn. The little dog seemed thrilled to see them all: her tail wagged triple-time and she was so excited that she sneezed three times in a row.

I've been so lonely! All I want is to be loved. And right now? I feel loved.

"Ohh, she's so soft!" said Maria when she knelt to pet Cuddles. "Aren't you a darling?"

"She's just like a stuffie toy," Lizzie said. "With those eyes, and that adorable fluffy fur." She couldn't get over how cute Cuddles was.

Poppy just sat down on the sidewalk and let Cuddles climb into her lap. She didn't say anything; she didn't have to. The smile on her face said it all.

CHAPTER SIX

Lizzie and Maria exchanged looks and smiles as they watched Poppy and Cuddles. It was obvious that Poppy really did love dogs—and that Cuddles loved kids. "How about that walk, then?" Lizzie finally asked.

Poppy gave Cuddles one more hug and stood up. "Can I hold her leash?" she asked.

"Sure," Lizzie said. She handed it to Poppy. "It looks like Cuddles already knows how to walk nicely on a leash."

"Unlike Misha," called Maria over her shoulder as the husky dragged her down the sidewalk.

Cuddles didn't pull on the leash. She wanted to take her time investigating her neighborhood. Lizzie and Poppy laughed as the fluffy pup zigged and zagged her way up the sidewalk, sniffing everything and wagging her little tail.

What a wonderful world! So many things to see and smell!

"She sure is happy to be off that porch," said Lizzie.

Poppy nodded. "She doesn't deserve to be cooped up that way. How old do you think she is? I would guess around six months."

"That's exactly what I would have said." Lizzie grinned at Poppy. "I wonder if she's full-grown yet or if she'll get any bigger."

"Well, from what I read online last night," said Poppy, "she probably won't grow too much more.

The whole idea with these dogs is that they're supposed to stay pretty small."

Lizzie was impressed. "So you've really looked into these teddy bear dogs," she said. She realized that she hadn't even taken the time yet to look up the breed. Maybe she had finally met someone who was even more dog-crazy than she was.

Poppy shrugged. "I was curious," she said. "There's always something to learn about dogs." Then she laughed out loud as she pointed to Cuddles, who was standing on her hind legs to sniff at the yellow flowers covering a bush at the end of someone's driveway. "Looks like someone else has a lot of curiosity, too."

"What else did you find out about teddy bear dogs?" Lizzie asked.

"Well, they're really sweet, and smart, and affectionate," said Poppy. "They're often a mix between a bichon frise and a Shih Tzu, so some people also call them Zuchon dogs."

"Cuddles looks more like she's part poodle," said Lizzie.

Poppy nodded eagerly. "That's what I thought, because of her coloring and her curly hair. Lots of teddy bear dogs do have poodle in them. And most of them are hypoallergenic, so even people like my mom who are allergic to dogs can have them." She stopped talking and kicked at a stone on the sidewalk. "Not that I could ever talk my mom into having a dog. I've tried. Last time I asked, she told me that the more I bugged her about it, the less likely we were to get a dog. So now I don't say a word." She pretended to zip her lip.

Lizzie felt bad for Poppy. Anyone could see how much this girl wanted a dog of her own. She decided to change the subject. "Hey, look at Cuddles," she said. "Where did she learn how to do that?"

Cuddles had found an old tennis ball, and she was pushing it along the sidewalk with her nose, like a soccer player moving the ball up the field. When she heard her name, she looked back at Lizzie and Poppy and gave them a happy grin.

Life is full of interesting things. Isn't it great?

"Agh! She's so adorable I can't stand it!" said Poppy.

"I know," said Lizzie. "She's one of those little dogs who make you understand why some people love little dogs."

Poppy laughed and gave Lizzie a high five. "Exactly," she said.

Misha dragged Maria back down the sidewalk toward Poppy and Lizzie. Maria handed Misha's leash to Lizzie. "It's your turn for this wacky dude," she said. "He's pulled me around long enough, and I have to go walk my own clients' dogs now." She bent down to give Cuddles one last kiss, then headed off.

"Can I try walking Misha?" Poppy asked Lizzie. "I read about an idea that might help with the pulling."

Lizzie shrugged and traded leashes with Poppy. "Be my guest," she said as she took Cuddles's leash. If Poppy could teach a husky not to pull, she really had dog magic.

Poppy started off down the sidewalk with Misha. Every time he started to pull, she stopped and turned the opposite way, then kept walking. That meant she was taking only a few steps at a time in any direction, but she didn't seem frustrated. She wore a look of concentration as she worked with the big strong fluffy dog.

"Hey, what's going on here?"

Lizzie turned to see Daphne walking down the sidewalk. She looked mad. "Misha is my responsibility," she said when she'd stopped in front of them, hands on hips. "I'm not supposed to let just anyone walk him, especially a little kid."

Poppy frowned. "I'm not a little kid," she said before Lizzie could say a word. "I'm almost eight. And I know how to walk dogs."

"Um, maybe I'd better take him," Lizzie said quietly. Poppy handed over Misha's leash, and Lizzie traded it for Cuddles's.

"What were you doing, anyway," Daphne asked, "going back and forth like that? You're getting Misha all mixed up." She glared at Poppy.

Poppy didn't back down. "It's a training technique I read about," she said. "It's a proven way to train dogs not to pull on the leash."

"Well, isn't that interesting," said Daphne. "Not." She took Misha's leash from Lizzie. "I'm back on duty," she said. "My aunt left this morning, so I'll take my route back, thank you very much." Then she finally seemed to notice Cuddles. "What, you added another dog to my list? I can barely handle all my clients as it is."

Cuddles cocked her head, looking from Daphne to Lizzie.

What's the problem here? I thought we were having fun!

Lizzie frowned. Why was Daphne being such a pain? "I'm walking Cuddles for free. And Poppy and I will keep doing it—you don't have to worry."

Daphne tossed her head. "Fine," she said. "Maybe you can teach her not to bark, too—since you're both such know-it-alls about dogs."

Poppy and Lizzie looked at each other and shrugged. "Maybe we can," said Poppy.

CHAPTER SEVEN

"So, Poppy knew about this method I never even heard of," Lizzie told her friends the next day. "It's called the whisper trick, and it's for teaching dogs not to bark."

Brianna and Maria looked interested, but Daphne rolled her eyes. The four of them were having their monthly business meeting, at Maria's house. They were in her room, sprawled on the thick rag rug next to her bed.

"What is your problem, Daphne?" Lizzie asked. "I think it's pretty impressive how much Poppy knows about dogs. You should see this whole report she did on teddy bear dogs, with pictures she downloaded and everything." Lizzie had totally given in to the idea that there was someone out there who knew more about dogs than she did. Poppy was amazing! She was like a walking, talking dog encyclopedia.

"I don't know, it's just annoying," said Daphne. "Plus, she's just dying to take over my route."

"Oh, come on," said Lizzie. "She's just a kid. I mean, maybe someday she could join our business, like as a junior member, but—"

Daphne looked like she was about to blow up, so Lizzie changed the subject. "Anyway, I think Poppy's cool. She wants to be an astronaut and go to Mars someday!"

"Yeah, well, there aren't any dogs in space," said Daphne.

"But there were!" Lizzie had to laugh, remembering how Poppy had told her all about a Russian program back in the 1950s and '60s in which dogs—and also mice and rats and rabbits—were rocketed into orbit around the earth. Lizzie told her friends about it. "She even knew the dogs' names! I'm not kidding, this girl knows more about dogs than anybody I've ever met."

"Really." Daphne raised an eyebrow.

"Really!" said Lizzie. "Her mom even had to make a rule that Poppy had to stop telling her dog facts. She said Poppy was driving her batty."

"See?" said Daphne. "She drives me batty, too. That's why I only let her come with me on my route a couple of times. She does nothing but talk about dogs, dogs, dogs."

Maria passed around the plate of oatmeal-raisin cookies her mom had made for their meeting. Lizzie could tell she was trying to make peace. "So what is this whisper trick, anyway?" Maria asked. "It's a new training thing? Maybe we should put it into our book." The girls always talked about writing the AAA Dynamic Dog Walkers dog-training book. They knew it would be a bestseller, but somehow they'd never really gotten much past talking about it.

"I think I've heard of it," said Brianna. "Isn't it when you teach a dog how to 'whisper,' like bark without sound, or at least really quietly? Then, when the dog is barking loudly, you tell them, 'whisper!' It helps them learn to tone it down."

"That's the one," said Lizzie. "Poppy and I are going to start trying it with Cuddles. I have a feeling she can learn it, too. That little dog is a big smartie."

The whole time Lizzie was talking, Daphne was staring at Brianna. "So now you're a big expert on dogs, too?" she asked.

Brianna shrugged. "I like learning about dogs," she said.

"And why do you have to teach Cuddles not to bark, anyway?" Daphne turned to Lizzie. "I thought you said she wouldn't bark anymore if she got more attention."

"Well, I guess she got in the habit of barking," said Lizzie. "Now she does it sometimes even when we're out walking."

Daphne smirked. "I guess you don't know everything about dogs after all," she said.

Lizzie shrugged. "I never said I did," she said. Why did Daphne have to act this way?

"Hey," said Maria, "I have an idea." She put down her cookie. "Why don't we have a contest, like a dog trivia contest? That way we can settle once and for all who knows the most about dogs."

Lizzie turned to stare at her friend. "That's the best idea ever," she said. Immediately, her brain started working overtime. "We could have it at Lucky Dog Books. I know Jerry Small would love it." Lizzie knew the owner of her favorite bookstore because he had adopted the rest of Buddy's family. Jerry Small was into anything that had to do with dogs.

"Awesome idea," said Brianna. "Maybe it could be, like, a fund-raiser. We could raise money for Caring Paws."

"We can enter the contest, right?" Daphne asked. "Even if we're the ones planning it?"

"Of course," Lizzie said. "Anyone can. And a fund-raiser is a great idea. We could charge admission, plus an entry fee for everybody who wants to be in the contest." She loved this whole idea. But she already knew she wasn't going to be just one of the contestants. She had a better idea.

"I want to be the one asking the questions!" she said. "I can do the research and come up with tons of dog trivia." She could hardly wait to get home to her room, with its bookshelves stuffed with every kind of dog book. She had breed books and training books and dog encyclopedias, not to mention a shelf full of picture books and novels about dogs. She could also go online to look for dog trivia questions.

This was going to be so much fun—especially when Poppy won the contest, which Lizzie knew she would. For one thing, Lizzie couldn't wait to see Daphne's face. Also, if Poppy won, maybe it would help convince her mom to foster—or even adopt—Cuddles. That was *Lizzie*'s great idea—but she wasn't ready to share it with anyone yet. First of all, she had to talk to Mrs. Bennett. Lizzie knew that Cuddles would be happier with Poppy and Allie, but Mrs. Bennett had to believe that, too.

Meeting Poppy had gotten Lizzie thinking about the time before Buddy, when she and her brothers wanted a dog so badly. She used to beg for a puppy all the time, but her parents had always said no. Then she'd had the brilliant idea of convincing them to at least foster puppies—and look what had happened since then! Not only had her family helped dozens of puppies, they had ended up with one of their own — once Lizzie and Charles had proven how responsible they could be. Why couldn't it work out the same way for Poppy?

CHAPTER EIGHT

The next day, Lizzie went straight to Allie and Poppy's house instead of stopping to pick up Misha. The big husky was Daphne's responsibility again.

"Ready to go get Cuddles?" she asked when Poppy answered the door.

Poppy nodded eagerly. "I finished all my schoolwork early today so we could take her for a nice long walk."

"Have fun," called Allie from the kitchen, where she was tapping away on her laptop. Lizzie had learned that Allie had an online business, helping to build websites. She was always busy on her computer.

"We will," Lizzie told Poppy's mom. "And I know Cuddles will be really happy to see Poppy."

They set off for Mrs. Bennett's house. Lizzie told Poppy about the trivia contest. "It's going to be such a blast," she said.

"It sounds like fun," said Poppy. "Maybe I'll enter the contest."

"You have to!" said Lizzie. "You know more about dogs than anyone! You're practically guaranteed—" she stopped herself. She didn't want to get Poppy's hopes up, even though she was sure Poppy would win. "You're guaranteed to have a good time," she finished.

She was dying to tell Poppy some of the fun facts she had already learned about dogs. She was really enjoying the job of coming up with questions for the trivia contest. The night before she'd spent hours in her room, surrounded by her dog books.

She'd learned all kinds of new facts, about the tallest dog in the world (the Great Dane), the smallest (Chihuahua), and the fluffiest (probably a keeshond). Poppy was right: there really was always something new to learn about dogs.

But she couldn't tell Poppy—of course she couldn't. If Poppy knew the answers to the trivia questions—or even what the questions were going to be—that would be cheating. Lizzie knew that Poppy would win even without that kind of help. She probably already knew all those facts, anyway!

Lizzie also wanted to tell Poppy about her idea for Cuddles's new home—but she kept quiet about that, too.

Instead, she let Poppy chatter as they walked, mostly about what she planned to name all the dogs she dreamed of having. "The Dalmatian will be Spot, of course," she said, "and the husky will be Belka, after one of those Russian dogs who went

into space. I think I'll name my Great Dane something like Jefferson, or Napoleon. Like a really
serious name for a big dog." She looked off into the
distance, dreamy-eyed. Lizzie could tell that she
was picturing each dog in her mind.

Cuddles started to bark and bounce and run
up and down the porch as soon as Lizzie and
Poppy got near the green house.

*Yay! I've been waiting and waiting and waiting
for you! And now you're here. Yay!*

Lizzie tried to calm the fluffy pup so she could
clip on her leash. Cuddles was too excited. She
dashed around Lizzie's feet in a wild happy dance.
"Hey, come here," said Lizzie. "Sit!"

Cuddles ignored her and kept jumping and
twirling and barking. She sneezed three times,
adorable tiny sneezes.

Poppy knelt near the puppy and stroked her soft fur gently, whispering comforting words. Soon Cuddles was curled in Poppy's lap, relaxed and happy.

"Whew!" said Lizzie. "She sure is a bundle of energy."

"But she knows how to calm down, too," said Poppy. "All she needs is a little love." She held the tiny dog up and kissed the top of her head. "Okay, you can put the leash on now."

They began to walk around the block, Cuddles leading the way with her tail wagging like a miniature flag.

Look at me, everyone! Enjoy the cuteness!

A few minutes later, she stopped to bark at a cat in someone's yard. Lizzie put her hands over her ears. She had learned to like small dogs, but she could never get used to their high-pitched yippy barking. "Weren't we going to work on this?" she asked Poppy. "How do we teach her to whisper?"

"From what I read, it could take some time," said Poppy. "But I'm sure it will work. The first step is to teach her to bark on command. Like when she's already barking anyway, we tell her, 'Speak!' and give her a treat. That helps her understand what 'speak' means."

Lizzie pulled a tiny treat out of her pocket. "Cuddles, speak!" she said while Cuddles barked. Cuddles stopped barking for a second and cocked her adorable head.

Huh? I'm kinda busy here. What did you want?

Lizzie waited until Cuddles started to bark again. "Good girl," said Lizzie. "Speak!" She gave Cuddles the treat. Then they headed off down the block. The next time Cuddles began to bark—at a mailman walking down the sidewalk—Lizzie tried it again. "Speak, Cuddles!" she said, over Cuddles's barking. She tossed her a treat. "Good girl," she said.

Cuddles sat down to chew the treat daintily. When she finished, she gazed up at Lizzie and barked again. "Good speak!" Lizzie laughed as she gave Cuddles another treat. This dog caught on quickly!

Cuddles barked again and again, wagging her tail happily.

Wow! I'm getting rewarded for barking, instead of getting yelled at! I love this game.

"Okay, that's fun—what next?" Lizzie asked when they had walked all the way around the block. Now they were standing in front of Poppy's house.

"Well, you would do that for a few days," said Poppy. "Then you start teaching her to 'whisper' instead of 'speak.' You say it in a tiny voice so she gets the idea. You can hold your finger to your lips as a signal, too. You wait until she barks a little more softly, then tell her, 'Good whisper!' and give her the treat." She shrugged. "It won't happen overnight, but I guess most dogs can learn to bark really, really quietly."

Lizzie nodded. "Sounds great," she said. More than ever, she wished Poppy could foster or even adopt Cuddles. Think of all the things this smart pup could learn from such a good trainer!

"Hey! Catch him!" Lizzie turned to see who was shouting. It was Daphne, racing down the sidewalk after Misha. The big furry husky was tearing along with his leash dragging behind him. "He spotted a squirrel and he took off!" Daphne said, panting, as she ran up to Lizzie and

Poppy. Misha had veered off into someone's yard and was staring up at a tree. "When he gets free, he's impossible to catch—he just dances away from anyone who gets near. What if he runs into the street?"

Daphne looked so upset that Lizzie's heart went out to her. Sometimes it was really scary to be responsible for someone else's dog.

Poppy handed Cuddles's leash to Lizzie. "I think I know how to get him," she said.

CHAPTER NINE

Poppy took off running — into her own backyard. "Misha!" she kept calling. "This way!" She stuck two fingers into her mouth and whistled a loud piercing whistle.

"Wow," said Lizzie as she and Daphne ran that way, too. "I always wanted to be able to whistle like that. And look! He heard her and he's interested."

Misha stood like a statue, his head cocked and his ears pricked high. He looked around, sniffing at the air, as if trying to figure out where the noises came from.

"Misha!" yelled Poppy again. She stood in her backyard, waving her arms to catch his attention.

"This way!" And then, as Misha started to move toward her, she did something amazing. She ran away from him, dodging between the swing set and a flower garden.

"What's she doing?" Daphne asked. "I thought she was going to help catch him."

Lizzie laughed. "She's doing exactly the right thing. She's making herself more interesting than a squirrel. She has to grab Misha's attention before we can grab him."

Lizzie knew the 'running away' trick. It worked just about every time. "Dogs are curious creatures," her aunt Amanda had told her. "When they hear or see something interesting, they want to check it out."

Sure enough, Misha galloped into Poppy's backyard. Lizzie and Daphne ran, too, with Cuddles twinkling along beside them. They arrived just in time to see Poppy petting Misha's side. "Good boy," she was saying as she moved slowly to take hold of the panting husky's trailing leash. "What a good boy, Misha!"

Misha wagged and wriggled and grinned up at her. He didn't seem to mind being caught—not when the dogcatcher was so nice. Lizzie could see how happy Misha was that Poppy knew how to scratch him in the exact right spot between the ears.

The back door of the Bauers' house popped open and Allie stepped out. "What's going on out here? Dogs and kids tearing all over the yard!"

"Poppy caught Misha!" Daphne said. "That was awesome, Poppy."

Lizzie's eyebrows shot up. That was the first nice thing Daphne had said to Poppy.

Daphne noticed. "What?" she asked. "It was great. You really are terrific with dogs, Poppy. Thank you!"

She walked over and took Misha's leash from Poppy. "But don't think it means I'm not going to beat you at that trivia contest!" she added with a smile as she headed off down the sidewalk.

"It looks great in here, don't you think?" Lizzie asked Maria. She spun around to admire the dog-themed decorating they'd done, along with Daphne and Brianna and Jerry Small. Allie and Poppy had helped, too. They had all worked hard to put the trivia contest together, and now, a week later, it was almost time for it to begin.

Cuddles was the guest of honor, and she had spent the afternoon racing up and down the aisles of Lucky Dog Books, accepting cookies whenever she did something cute (which happened, Lizzie thought, about every two seconds) and whisper-barking the way Poppy had taught her.

It was the best trick ever! It was so cute. Cuddles

would start barking because something exciting was happening, like when people were blowing up balloons. Poppy would put her finger to her mouth and say, "Whisper, Cuddles," and the puppy's shrill barks would fade to tiny whimpers you could barely hear. She looked proud of herself when Poppy told her what a good girl she was.

I'm a quick study! Teach me some more tricks!

Lizzie couldn't wait to try teaching the whisper trick to a few other barking dogs she knew. Meanwhile, tonight was the big night, and she was ready. Or was she? The contestants and the audience would be arriving any minute, and suddenly, Lizzie was nervous.

She taped up one last poster, of a litter of adorable pug puppies sitting in a blue wheelbarrow, then sat down to check her stack of questions one more time. She had written them all out on color-coded index cards: yellow for easy, blue for medium, and red for really hard questions. She planned to start with easy questions, like—she shuffled her cards and picked one out—"What is a dog's most powerful sense?" Most people knew that dogs had an incredible sense of smell, so they would probably guess that—and they'd be right.

The way the contest worked was Lizzie would ask each contestant a question in turn. If they answered correctly, they stayed in. If not, they were out. "That way," Jerry Small had suggested, "Dog Trivia Night won't go on all night long."

Lizzie glanced up to see that the room was filling with people. Her aunt Amanda was there, and so was Ms. Dobbins. They were going to be tough contestants, since both of them knew so much about dogs. Lizzie's parents and brothers were there, and Poppy's mom, and lots of other families.

Besides Maria, Brianna, Daphne, and Poppy, there was a sprinkling of other kids lining up to enter the contest. And almost all the seats in the audience—the rows of chairs Lizzie had helped set up—were already filled. Maria had done a good job advertising the contest, putting up dozens of copies of the poster she and Brianna had designed.

The bookstore was packed—which meant they'd be raising a lot of money for Caring Paws.

Lizzie looked around to see if Mrs. Bennett had come. There she was, in the back. Lizzie smiled and waved, and Mrs. Bennett waved back. Lizzie was glad she had taken a moment to have a private talk with Mrs. Bennett the day before. She had agreed to let Poppy and her mom take

Cuddles—if Allie agreed. "They live so close," she said. "I can see their yard from my window, so Cuddles would still be in my sight, just like I promised my sister."

Lizzie looked at Poppy, who was holding Cuddles on her lap. They'd planned to have Poppy introduce the tiny pup to the audience before the contest began. The two of them looked perfect together. Poppy needed Cuddles in her life as much as Cuddles needed Poppy. *Now*, thought Lizzie, *all we have to do is convince her mom.* And how hard could that be, once Poppy won the contest?

CHAPTER TEN

"Welcome to our first Dog Trivia Night!" Jerry Small stood in front of the audience, smiling broadly. "It's so great to see you all. Before we start, I want to introduce you to our special guest, Cuddles." He gestured to the stage, where Poppy stood holding Cuddles's leash.

The audience broke into applause and cheers. Cuddles joined in, barking at the top of her lungs. After the clapping stopped, she was still barking.

"Whisper, Cuddles," said Poppy, holding her finger over her own mouth.

Cuddles looked up at Poppy, wagging her tail. Her barking dropped to a whisper.

I can do it! See? I can do it!

"Good girl!" Poppy said, and the audience cheered and applauded all over again—which made Cuddles start barking again, which made the audience crack up.

As soon as Poppy got Cuddles whispering again, Jerry Small stepped in. "What a great trick," he said. "And now, on with the show."

Lizzie's mom came to take Cuddles's leash, as they'd arranged. Then Jerry Small waved Lizzie to the front. "Lizzie Peterson is our emcee tonight. She'll be asking the questions, and our wonderful group of experts will do their best to stay in the game. The winner will receive a gift certificate to Lucky Dog Books, and all the money raised tonight will go to Caring Paws." Quickly, he introduced the contestants, all fifteen of them.

Lizzie stood nervously, holding her index cards. She felt better when she saw Aunt Amanda smile at her. And then it was time to ask the first question. She faced Brianna, the first person in the line of contestants. "True or false," she said, reading off a yellow card. "Dogs are color-blind."

"True!" Brianna said, almost before Lizzie had finished speaking.

"Correct," said Lizzie, smiling at her friend. From that moment on, she lost her nervousness and enjoyed her role onstage.

She was surprised at how many adults went out in the first round. How could anybody not know that the poodle is the national dog of France, or that the Labrador retriever is the most popular dog in the United States?

By the second round, when she began to read off her blue index cards, there were only eight contestants left. Daphne and Poppy were both still in the game, but Maria had gone out on her first yellow-card question. "Black?" she had guessed when Lizzie asked her what color Dalmatians were at birth. Lizzie shook her head sadly and passed the question to Brianna, who knew that the spotted dogs started out all white.

Lizzie faced Aunt Amanda. "Are domesticated dogs carnivores, omnivores, or herbivores?" she asked. She knew her aunt would get this one right.

Sure enough, Aunt Amanda knew that dogs were omnivores, who eat both meat and vegetables. She got a laugh from the audience when she said, "At least my dog Bowser is. He'll eat just about anything!"

Brianna stayed in the game by answering "dachshund" when Lizzie asked what dogs were bred to chase rabbits out of holes. Then Lizzie asked Poppy what the nickname was for the dogs commonly known as Mexican hairless. Poppy was ready with the answer.

"Xolo," she said, pronouncing it like "show-low." "But don't ask me to pronounce the real name."

"Xolo is correct!" Lizzie nodded, looking down at the card in her hand. "I didn't know how to pronounce the whole name, either, but I learned the other night. The full name is spelled—" she took a deep breath—"X-o-l-o-i-t-z-c-u-i-n-t-l-i, and you say it like 'show-low-itz-kweent-lee.'"

The audience laughed and applauded.

Then something surprising happened. Daphne missed a question. "Alaska," she said when Lizzie asked where the Siberian husky originated.

There was a groan from the audience.

"I'm sorry," said Lizzie, and she really was sorry, since Daphne looked so crushed. "But they originated in a part of Russia called Siberia."

"I thought it was a trick question!" Daphne wailed.

After that, it was down to Poppy, Brianna, and Aunt Amanda. Aunt Amanda went down on her next question, which Lizzie read off a red index card. "What is the word for 'fear of dogs'?"

Aunt Amanda looked blankly at Lizzie. She shrugged. "No idea," she said.

"Cynophobia," Poppy said without missing a beat when Lizzie passed the question to her.

That made the crowd applaud. Lizzie could tell they all wanted Poppy to win. Everyone could see how smart she was and how passionate about dogs she was. She was cute, too, with those Pippi Longstocking braids.

Lizzie noticed that Brianna stood quietly, looking down at her feet. Brianna obviously knew that Poppy was the crowd favorite, but she didn't let it stop her from getting her next question right, the one about another name for the Russian wolfhound. "Borzoi," she said, still looking at her feet.

It was Poppy's turn again. Lizzie could see the people in the audience leaning forward. This was exciting.

"How many teeth does a dog have?" Lizzie asked.

"Oh, I know this one," said Poppy, biting her lip. "I know I do." She seemed unsure. "Forty-six?"

Lizzie checked the answer. "Um, no!" she said, shocked.

The audience gasped. Everyone turned to stare at Brianna. If she got the answer right, she would win.

"Brianna?" Lizzie asked. "Would you like me to repeat the question?"

Brianna shook her head. "That's okay." She looked straight back at Lizzie this time instead of at her shoes. "A healthy adult dog has forty-two teeth: twenty on the upper jaw and twenty-two on the lower jaw." She said it shyly, as if she didn't want to show off.

"Correct!" said Lizzie. She saw Brianna's face turn white, then pink as the audience hooted and cheered. She also saw a very upset Poppy jump up and run down one of the aisles until she disappeared into the back of the store.

As soon as she was done congratulating Brianna, Lizzie took Cuddles's leash from her mom and ran with her to find Poppy. The red-haired girl was huddled near the cozy corner where Jerry Small kept all his dog books. She was sobbing into a black Lab stuffie who lived there.

"It's okay, Poppy," Lizzie said as she stroked Poppy's shoulder. "You did great."

Cuddles snuggled into Poppy's lap and licked at her salty tears.

Please don't cry! I'll make you feel better.

"But—but I thought if I won, maybe my mom would let me have a dog," Poppy said. "I thought she might let me have *this* dog. I thought she might let me at least foster Cuddles."

Lizzie couldn't believe that Poppy had been thinking the same way she had—though it made sense, since they were so alike in so many ways. But before she could tell Poppy she'd had a similar idea, she heard someone speak up behind her.

"She might let you anyway," said the someone. It was Allie, Poppy's mom. "Sweetie." She knelt to hug Poppy. "You were amazing. And not just tonight. You were amazing when you caught Misha, and when you taught Cuddles her whisper trick, and just the way you stuck to it when you and Lizzie promised to help Cuddles. You've proved to me how responsible you can be."

"Really?" Poppy asked.

"Really," said her mom. "And Cuddles is amazing, too. I think the two of you belong together—forever. Plus, I've kind of fallen in love with her myself. She's just so cuddly! I've already talked to Mrs. Bennett about it, and she thinks it's a great idea for us to adopt Cuddles. We can make room in our life for one tiny dog, right? Especially one I won't be allergic to?"

Poppy hugged her mom tight. She didn't have to say anything. Once again, her face said it all.

Lizzie beamed. This was a hundred times better than convincing Allie to foster Cuddles. Now the adorable pup would be with Poppy forever, and they'd both be where Lizzie could visit them anytime. "I think you won first prize after all," she told Poppy as the little girl hugged her new puppy close. "And I think Cuddles did, too."

PUPPY TIPS

I hear from a lot of readers who, like Poppy, really want a dog of their own. Sometimes there are very good reasons why it's not the right time for a family to add a dog to their lives: for example if parents are too busy with work, or dogs are not allowed where you live, or someone in your family is allergic. If one of these is true for your family, maybe you can find a place like Caring Paws to volunteer with dogs, or perhaps a neighbor or friend has a dog that you could help out with. That way, you can spend time with dogs and begin to learn about how to take care of one of your own when the time is right. (It might also help convince your parents that you can be a responsible dog owner!)

Dear Reader,

It's fun to learn about dogs, and there's so much to know! Your library probably has books about dog breeds, dog training, and dog care. That's a great place to start. You can also look online if you're interested in a particular breed or training issue. Your parents can help you track down what you want to know. I do a lot of research when I'm writing the Puppy Place books, and I never get tired of learning about dogs. For this book, I enjoyed researching the questions that Lizzie would ask at the trivia contest!

Yours from the Puppy Place,

Ellen Miles

DON'T MISS THE
NEXT PUPPY PLACE
ADVENTURE!

Here's a peek at Bentley

Charles gazed out the car window down a long valley filled with trees in shades of rosy red, bright yellow, and burnt orange. They looked like giant bouquets. The grass was still a fresh green, like spring, but the leaves were in full-autumn bloom. The colors were beautiful, but Charles couldn't wait for the road to start climbing out of the valley. He couldn't wait to breathe the crisp, mountain air. He knew his puppy, Buddy, was super excited, too. The Petersons were off to the mountains for the weekend!

Was Lizzie excited? Charles wasn't so sure about his older sister. The trip was all because of her, but she was very quiet. She sat on the other side of the backseat, counting on her fingers. Every once in a while, she pulled a carefully folded sheet of paper from the pocket of her purple fleece jacket. Charles knew it was a checklist. Lizzie had been carrying it around for a week, ever since her last Greenies meeting.

Greenies was the name of Lizzie's nature club. Lizzie was in it with her best friend, Maria, and a bunch of older kids from their school. Even though Charles was not a member of the Greenies, he had been invited on the club's big annual camping trip to Misty Valley. Mom and Dad were invited, too!

So was the Bean, Charles's younger brother, but he was staying with Aunt Amanda for the weekend. Charles was sure the Bean didn't mind—in fact, he was probably very happy, since Aunt Amanda had a house full of animals. Charles wrapped his arm around Buddy's neck and looked back out the window. He was pretty happy, too. But Lizzie was still looking very serious.

"Why are you so worried?" Charles asked.

"What?" Lizzie asked. "Who me? Why do you think I'm worried?"

Charles shrugged. "Because you keep staring at that paper and mumbling to yourself."

"This paper happens to be my checklist," Lizzie explained.

"Yeah, but you already checked everything off, like fifteen times," Charles pointed out.

"I'm just making sure," said Lizzie. "And besides, all the knots I need to know are on the

other side. Plus the words to a new camp song."
Lizzie had a special rope at home, just for practic-
ing tying knots. She looped it around the end of
her bed, the leg of a chair, anywhere. Sometimes,
she would sing camp songs while she practiced.

"I thought camping was supposed to be fun,"
Charles said.

"It is," Lizzie said. "But remember, the Greenies
don't get to stay in cabins like you do. We won't
have running water or electricity or beds. We'll
get our water from a nearby stream and cook our
own food and put our tents up all by ourselves.
The Greenies are doing real camping."

Lizzie sometimes acted like a know-it-all, but
Charles knew she had never done camping like
this before. He could tell she was nervous.

ABOUT THE AUTHOR

Ellen Miles loves dogs, which is why she has a great time writing the Puppy Place books. And guess what? She loves cats, too! (In fact, her very first pet was a beautiful tortoiseshell cat named Jenny.) That's why she came up with the Kitty Corner series. Ellen lives in Vermont and loves to be outdoors with her dog, Zipper, every day, walking, biking, skiing, or swimming, depending on the season. She also loves to read, cook, explore her beautiful state, play with dogs, and hang out with friends and family.

Visit Ellen at ellenmiles.net.